092016

A   Auch, Mary Jane
             Eggs mark the spot.

EGGS
MARK THE SPOT

written and illustrated by
Mary Jane Auch

Holiday House/New York

Pauline was a hen with a special talent. If she concentrated on a flower as she laid an egg, a perfect image of that flower would appear on the egg's surface. Pauline could copy absolutely anything. Her eggs were extraordinary. She lived a simple life on Mrs. Pennywort's farm, but stories about the hen who could lay decorated eggs had spread far and wide.

For John and Kate Briggs

Copyright © 1996 by Mary Jane Auch
All rights reserved
Printed in the United States of America
First Edition

Library of Congress Cataloging-in-Publication Data
Auch, Mary Jane.
Eggs mark the spot / written and illustrated by Mary Jane Auch.
p.   cm.
Summary: Pauline the hen uses her talent for laying eggs with the image of what she sees to help capture the thief who has stolen a famous painting from an art gallery.
ISBN 0-8234-1242-3 (hardcover : alk. paper)
[1. Chickens—Fiction.   2. Painting—Fiction.   3. Robbers and outlaws—Fiction.]   I. Title.
PZ7.A898Eg   1996   95-44930   CIP   AC
[E]—dc20

One day, the director of the Big City Art Gallery called Mrs. Pennywort. "We have a new exhibit of paintings by world-famous artists," she said. "We've heard about your amazing hen, and we'd like her to lay one egg for each of the paintings. Do you think she's up to the task?"

"Sure," said Mrs. Pennywort. "You name it, Pauline can copy it."

"Wonderful," said the gallery director. "We'll expect you here on Monday."

Pauline was excited about her assignment. But when she and Mrs. Pennywort got to the gallery, there was a problem. The art gallery was so crowded, Pauline could barely see the paintings. So how could she copy them? Even worse, the people couldn't see Pauline. °°Watch where you're going! Please!°° she clucked, but the humans couldn't understand Henspeak.

"The deal's off," Mrs. Pennywort told the director. "Poor Pauline is getting clobbered by all those big feet."

"But we did so want Pauline's special eggs," said the director. "Perhaps if we let her come back tonight when the gallery is closed . . ."

"Great idea," said Mrs. Pennywort. "We'll go pack our overnight bags."

"You don't need to come with your hen," said the director. "We'll take good care of her."

"Pauline's never been on a sleepover," said Mrs. Pennywort. "It's both of us or nothing."

When they went home, Mrs. Pennywort packed while Pauline took a nap. Later that night, they returned to the art gallery, and the guard let them in. At first, Pauline was overwhelmed by the wonderful works of art. She wandered from painting to painting, trying to decide which one to copy first.

Mrs. Pennywort yawned. "It's way past my bedtime, Pauline. I'll be in the next room if you need me. I spotted a nice bench I can sleep on in the Egyptian exhibit."

Soon Mrs. Pennywort's snores echoed through the marble building. The only other sounds were the guard's footsteps as he went on his rounds. He stopped to visit Pauline. "How are you doing, little lady?" he asked. "I'll bring you a treat on my next round."

Pauline settled in front of a painting by Modigliani. She carefully studied the shapes and colors until something began to look familiar. °°This painting reminds me of Mrs. Pennywort!°°

Then she concentrated and laid an egg.

Amedeo Modigliani, *Madame Zborowska with Clasped Hands*, c. 1917

°°Oh, my goodness,°° Pauline said, as she gazed at it. °°This isn't just
a copy. This is my own original design!°°

Henri Matisse, *The Rumanian Blouse*, 1940

Poulette moved on to a painting by a man named Matisse . . .

. . . and laid another egg.

Then she studied a Van Gogh . . .

Vincent Van Gogh, *L'Arlésienne (Mme. Ginoux)*, 1888

. . . and laid still another egg.

She looked at a Picasso . . .

Pablo Picasso, *9.1.38*, 1938

Paul Klee, *Clown*, 1929

. . . and a Klee, getting
more creative with each egg.

Pauline loved all of the paintings, but one of them really fluffed her feathers. It was a ballet dancer by Degas. She stared at it as Mrs. Pennywort came into the room.

"Just wanted to see how you're doing," Mrs. Pennywort said, picking up the first egg. "Pauline, this doesn't look exactly like the painting. Neither does this one. You're going to get us both in big trouble. Now stop messing around and just copy the pictures . . . perfectly! I'm going back to bed."

Pauline was devastated. °°Making up my own paintings was much more fun than just copying.°°

Later, when the guard came by with some sunflower-seed crackers, Pauline couldn't eat a crumb. "What's the matter?" he asked. "Where are those special eggs you're so famous for?"

°°You try to lay an egg when you're depressed!°° Pauline clucked. She concentrated on the Degas, trying to make a perfect copy, but her creative spirit was crushed.

The guard had just left when Pauline saw something out of the corner of her eye. At first she thought it was a huge spider. Then she realized it was a person—a man dressed all in black—coming down a rope from the skylight.

Hiding behind a statue, Pauline watched as the thief went straight for the Degas. He took the painting from the wall and started back up the rope. °°Put that down!°° squawked Pauline. °°That's my favorite painting!°°

Startled, the thief fell back to the floor, letting go of the painting. Pauline flew at his face, clamped her beak on the mask and pulled it off. The thief and the hen stared at each other for a long moment before they were interrupted.

"Hold on, Pauline, Mummy's coming!" Mrs. Pennywort yelled as she stumbled into the room. She had heard Pauline's squawk, but couldn't see very well without her glasses.

"It's the mummy from the Egyptian room!" screamed the thief when he saw Mrs. Pennywort. "It's alive!" He grabbed the painting and scrambled up the rope so fast, the skylight slammed shut on his foot.

All the commotion brought the guard running. "What's wrong?"
"I think someone was in here. Look! Poor Pauline is scared stiff," said
Mrs. Pennywort, patting a statue.

Pauline rushed over to the empty spot on the wall, flapping her wings and squawking. °°A thief stole the Degas!°°

"The Degas!" cried the gallery director. "It's missing!"

°°I just said that,°° clucked Pauline.

Soon the art gallery was filled with police. They scoured the area for clues, but found nothing.

"If only we had a witness," moaned the gallery director.

°°I'm a witness,°° said Pauline. °°I saw everything.°°

"How did he get in?" asked the guard. "I checked all the entrances."
°°Try the skylight,°° clucked Pauline.

"Whoever he is, he's clever," said the chief of police. "He got away without a trace."

°°No he didn't. He's still here!°° squawked Pauline, but nobody understood. She stared at the skylight, concentrating very hard.

Meanwhile, Mrs. Pennywort had unstuck the zipper on her sleeping bag and found her glasses. "Pauline, are you all right?" She picked up the egg Pauline had just laid. "This doesn't look like any of the paintings. Are you still messing around?"

°°People can be so dumb!°° clucked Pauline. °°Do I have to draw a diagram?°°

Pauline gathered her energy and laid three eggs under the skylight. Mrs. Pennywort rushed over. "I think Pauline is trying to tell us something. Look at her eggs."

°°Duh!°° said Pauline.

"The thief must have come down on a rope from the skylight," said the gallery director. "Then he grabbed the painting and escaped the same way. Pauline's eggs mark the spot."

They all looked up. "His foot is caught!" shouted the guard. "He's still here."

°°Double duh!°° clucked Pauline.

The police went to the roof, captured the thief and returned the Degas. Then the gallery director put the painting back in its frame. "Pauline, you're wonderful," she said. "You've saved the day . . . And you've saved the Degas!"

The police chief held up a perfect egg portrait of the thief. "This will make a great piece of evidence. We could use that chicken on the police force."

"Well, at least Pauline did something right," said Mrs. Pennywort, holding out the other eggs, "even though she didn't do a very good job of copying the paintings."

The art gallery director examined Pauline's eggs one by one. "But these are wonderful," she said. "Don't you see? Pauline has made her own original works of art, using the paintings for inspiration."

A few weeks later Pauline was invited to the art gallery again. Crowds pushed through the doors for the opening night of the new exhibit. But this time nobody stepped on Pauline.

After all, she *was* the featured artist.